BLITZ

More great reads in the
SHARP SHADES 2.0 *series:*

Sea Fever *by Gillian Philip*
Tears of a Friend *by Jo Cotterill*
Doing the Double *by Alan Durant*
A Murder of Crows *by Penny Bates*
Wrong Exit *by Mary Chapman*
Plague *by David Orme*
The Messenger *by John Townsend*
Witness *by Anne Cassidy*
Shouting at the Stars *by David Belbin*
Hunter's Moon *by John Townsend*
Who Cares? *by Helen Orme*

F
ORM

BLITZ

" At last I turned into Harrow Street. The school was still there. The houses opposite weren't.

Nothing but a pile of bricks and broken window frames. No number 18. And no Aunt Josie. And Aunt Josie had never believed in shelters. "

Bury College
Millennium LRC

BLITZ

David Orme

Ransom

SHARP SHADES 2.0
Blitz
by David Orme

Published by Ransom Publishing Ltd.
Radley House, 8 St. Cross Road, Winchester, Hampshire SO23 9HX, UK
www.ransom.co.uk

ISBN   978 178127 217 6
First published in 2007
This updated edition published by Ransom Publishing 2013

CONTENTS

1 Evacuee   9

2 Harrow Street   12

3 The Shelter   19

4 Back on the Train   24

5 Amnesia   32

6 Chickens   41

7 Hilda Will Know   47

8 A House Full of Aunts   55

7

CHAPTER ONE

Evacuee

People say I've fallen on my feet. I'm in the country. I have my own room. Bacon and eggs for breakfast. Back in London, bombs keep falling. Food is hard to get.

Outside, Auntie Minnie feeds the chickens. She makes a clucking sound with her mouth. Auntie Minnie is like an old mother hen. I'm one of her chickens.

Auntie Minnie and Uncle Trevor are too old to be my real aunt and uncle. They never had kids of their own. And that's the trouble. They can't do enough for me. I'm used to doing things for myself.

I feel like I'm wrapped in a big blanket. It's choking me to death.

The other evacuees think I'm mad when I complain. Every morning

they snigger when Auntie Minnie
walks me to school. I'm not going to
get lost. There's only one road in the
whole place.

OK, I know I'm cosy and well fed.
I know that people back in London
are going through hell. But I have to
get back there.

CHAPTER TWO

Harrow Street

I gave a note to my mate Charlie to give to Minnie. In the note, I said there was an emergency. I had to go to London. I would be back soon.

I told the teacher I was feeling

sick. She let me out an hour early. On the main road, I hitched a lift into Winchester.

It was late when I got to the train station. I asked the guard for a single ticket to London.

'Why are you going to London on your own?' the guard asked.

'I'm going to collect my little sister,' I lied. 'She isn't big enough to travel on her own.'

'Why are you only buying a single ticket then?'

'My mum will buy my ticket to come back with.'

'Why can't she bring your sister

down?'

' 'Cos of her war work. It's important. There is a war on, you know.'

It was a great day for telling porky-pies. I didn't have a sister, and my mum was dead. But my lies worked. I got the last train.

The journey took six hours.

There were air raids all night. The train hung around outside London for ages.

When I got out of the station I didn't know where I was. I'd only been away for a month. It was a mess then. Now everything had changed. The railway offices were flattened. The air was full of smoke. I crossed over Waterloo Road. I turned left along The Cut.

The shops on The Cut had their windows blown in. People were sweeping up glass and shovelling it into buckets. A copper was on the lookout for looters. He looked me up and down. There weren't many kids in London in 1940. Most of them were safely out in the country, eating bacon and eggs for breakfast. Sensible kids, not stupid ones like me. At last I turned into Harrow

Street. The school was still there. The houses opposite weren't. Nothing but a pile of bricks and broken window frames. No number 18. And no Aunt Josie. And Aunt Josie had never believed in shelters.

'No Adolf Hitler is going to drive me out of me own home!' she used to say.

CHAPTER THREE

The Shelter

I had no idea what to do. I was counting on Aunt Josie and Uncle Ted. Aunt Josie would give me one of her great, fat cuddles. She did this before, when Mum and Dad were killed.

'I'll be your mum now,' she had said. I hung around in Borough most of the day. I dodged the coppers. I wished I was older, like my cousin Stan. He was giving Hitler a bloody nose. By the time I was old enough to join up, it'd all be over.

I spent my last bob on pie and chips in the British Restaurant. I didn't even have the train fare back to Winchester.

As the evening grew dark, streams of people left the High Street. An old woman stopped me.

'What you doing out by yourself?' she asked.

'Bombed out,' I said.

'What, family gone? You'd better come along with me, darlin'.'

'Where to?'

'Borough Tube Station. They've opened it up as a shelter. Better hurry if you want a place to sleep.'

The station was packed solid with people. A dirty old bit of tunnel had been opened up to use as a shelter. It was lit by a few light bulbs. People kept bumping into each other. At last we got sorted out with a bunk. Then we had a sing-song.

The sing-song ended. Somewhere

up the tunnel, an old drunk carried on singing. At last someone shut him up. I think they chucked a boot at him.

At half-past six I followed people up the stairs. It was grey and drizzly. I had to go back to Harrow Street, but I didn't know why. I had no idea what I was going to do.

What had happened to Aunt Josie? I didn't want to think about it, but I had to. Then I heard a voice.

'Martin? What the 'ell are you doing back 'ere?'

CHAPTER FOUR

Back on the Train

It was Aunt Josie. I wept, even though I was too big for that sort of thing.

'I thought you were dead!' I said.

'I was round at Granny Hopkins'

when the bomb fell,' Auntie Josie
said. Then she started crying too.
But not before she said:

'Have you had any breakfast?'

We went to the British
Restaurant. I tucked into scrambled
eggs on toast. The eggs were made
from powdered egg. They were grey,
but they were hot.

I told Josie all about Auntie
Minnie and Uncle Trevor. I told her
how they fussed over me. Josie threw
her head back and gave one of her
great big fat laughs. She cheered up
the whole restaurant.

'I always said you were just like

your dad,' she said. 'He was Mr Independence when we were kids. Wouldn't be told anything.

'The thing is, Martin, what are we going to do now?'

She told me that she and Uncle Ted were staying with Hilda Levy, a few doors down. There was no room for me at Hilda's. It was too small.

Uncle Ted was a key man at the big railway works. He kept the engines running. He had to live nearby so he could get to work if there was an emergency. They couldn't just move away.

Uncle Ted was on an early shift

that day. He got home around four. We went to Waterloo. Ted went off to get a ticket. He came back and put it in my hand.

'It's a single ticket, OK? So stay where you're put, lad.'

'It's all for the best, Martin,' Aunt Josie said. She put some coins into my hand. Then we went to the Post Office to send a telegram to Auntie Minnie. She would be worried about me.

The train was late. It was nearly nine when we left. This time, I didn't look out of the window. It was dark and the blinds were down. The train was full of men in uniform. They were all smoking like mad.

'Glad to be away from London tonight,' a soldier said. 'Sky's clear. Someone's going to cop it.'

We stopped at Wimbledon. Suddenly, the siren started up. A raid! One of the soldiers woke up.

'Put your tin hats on, gents,' he said. Then he went to sleep again.

The train was stopped for ages. We could hear the sound of aircraft. I heard an explosion. Then came another, louder and closer. It made the whole train rock. Something hit me hard in the chest. There was a

blinding light. I was thrown out of my seat. I heard screams. A great weight was pressing down on me …

CHAPTER FIVE

Amnesia

'What's your name, dear?' the nurse asked.

I hadn't a clue. I was in hospital.

'How long have I been here?'

'You've been out cold for three

days. You're lucky. Apart from a lot
of bruises and sore ear-drums,
there's not much wrong with you.'

Later, I found out that they pulled
me out from under a stack of bodies
covered in blood. They thought I
was a goner.

But who was I? Bits of memories
floated round my head. They
seemed to be from long ago. I
remembered a face – my mum's face.
I remembered she was dead. I told
the nurse this.

'Who am I?'

'We don't know,' she said. 'All we
found in your pockets was a single

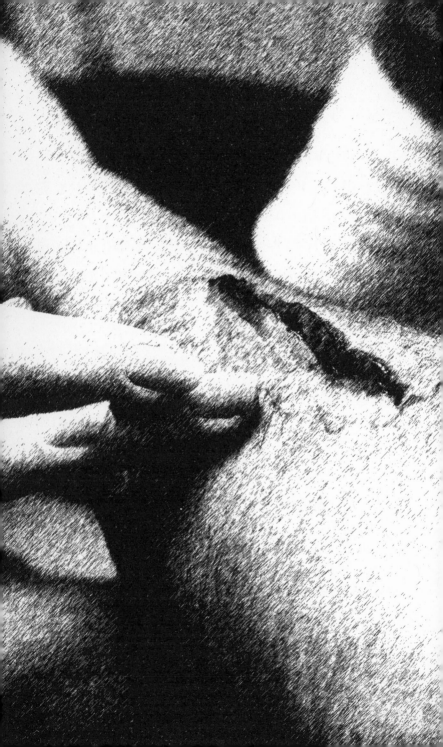

ticket to Winchester.'

Every night I heard sirens and the noise of guns and bombs. They scared me silly. I ended up shaking, with my head under the pillow.

It was ten days before I got out of bed. I still didn't know who I was. The hospital found me some second-hand clothes. They didn't want me hanging around any longer. They had really sick people to deal with.

A policeman came to see me. 'So which one are you?' he said. 'Frank Chipping or Ronald Drew?'

As far as I knew, I could be either.

Neither name rang any bells.

'I don't know,' I said. 'I can't remember.'

'You can't remember which one you are?'

I could see a trap heading my way.

'I don't know who I am. I just can't remember.'

A nurse came over. She went on about lots of people losing their memory in the raids. The copper wasn't having any of it.

'Two lads ran away from an orphanage on the night of the bomb,' he said. 'They were seen hanging about Waterloo Station.

This is one of them. He's made up a story about losing his memory.'

He glared at me again. 'There's a war on, sonny. We have better things to do than deal with liars. You'll be taken back this afternoon. Once you're there, stay where you're put!'

Stay where you're put. I remembered someone else saying those words to me. Not years ago but days ago. Who was it?

I sat and thought things out. I knew my mum and dad were dead. I could be Frank or Ronald. But I didn't like the sound of the orphanage. I had to get away before the police came to get me. Maybe I could find out who I was for myself.

I left the ward when nobody was looking. Soon I was in the entrance hall to the hospital. Loads of people were there. It was easy to slip out into the open air. When I was on the street I ran.

I had to get back to London. I had no money, so I would have to walk.

I walked a long way. I stopped at Putney. I was tired out and sore all over.

Then the sirens started up.

CHAPTER SIX

Chickens

I was scared. I didn't want to be out in the street. I wanted to be safe.

I pushed open a gate and ran up a path. I was in a garden. I could just make out a mound. I knew that shape. A shelter!

I pushed open the little door. It was pitch dark inside. I felt around and found a bunk. I got on it. Even though I was scared, I slept. I must have been weaker than I thought.

I woke up at dawn. I heard a sound. There were chickens outside. Someone was feeding them. She was making a clucking sound with her mouth. A clucking sound … Like Auntie Minnie … Who was Auntie Minnie? I remembered the cottage and Uncle Ted and the village school. That was where I belonged. Near Winchester. That was where my ticket was for!

I pushed open the shelter door. An old lady was feeding a run full of chickens. The old lady saw I was hungry. She gave me some breakfast.

'Where are you off to then?' the old lady said.

'Winchester.'

'By bus?'

I shook my head. 'I'm walking.'

'No money, eh? Come with me.'

We went back into the garden. She pulled a bike out of the shed and pushed it towards me. 'This was my son's. He's not coming back. It

might as well go to someone as can use it.'

I thanked her and pushed the bike out of the garden.

By midday I was at Waterloo Station. I left the bike by a wall. Someone would find it and be glad of it. I took the ticket to Winchester out of my pocket. There was a train due in half an hour.

I hung around for a bit, then headed for the barrier.

'Ticket, sonny.'

I held it out.

'This ticket's dated two weeks

ago! Where did you get this?'

A railway policeman came over. I looked round for somewhere to run to. No good. I was cornered. Then another voice called out.

'Martin? What the 'ell are you doin' back 'ere?'

CHAPTER SEVEN

Hilda Will Know

Martin? What the 'ell are you doin' back 'ere?

I knew those words so well. This wasn't the voice that said them last time. This voice belonged to a tall man in a railway uniform.

'D'you know this lad, then, Reg?' said the ticket collector.

'It's Ted Saunders' nephew. Seems every time they try and evacuate him he ends up back here … '

Reg, Ted Saunders, Josie Saunders. Aunt Josie … It was like a cork popping out of a shaken-up beer bottle. All my memories fizzed over. Martin? That was me! I knew who I was …

The next thing I knew I was flat out on a bed. Reg was looking down at me with a worried face. I tried to sit

up but I felt dizzy.

'Just lie still for a bit,' a woman's voice said.

It was a young woman. She was wearing a railway uniform too.

'I'm Margie,' she said. 'I'm the station first-aider. You fainted! When did you last eat?'

All the women I meet seem to think I need food. Funny thing is, they're always right. Some Marmite sandwiches appeared from nowhere. I ate them while I talked to Reg.

'What's happened to Uncle Ted and Aunt Josie? Why didn't they try and find me after the accident?'

'I don't know, Martin. I've been away for a couple of weeks. I only got back this morning. I haven't seen anything of Ted at all.'

I remembered Aunt Josie was looking for somewhere to live. They would have moved by now. I told Reg this.

'Hilda will know where they've moved to. I'll go round there.'

Reg nodded. 'All right, but come back if you get stuck.'

I went to the station entrance. Someone had nicked the bike. I set off to walk to Harrow Street.

Things seemed worse than last time. The city was smashed up.

It was almost dark when I turned in to Harrow Street. I got to Hilda Levy's house and banged on the door. I heard footsteps in the dark passage. The door opened. There was no light in the house, and no light in the street. I knew it was Hilda, but she couldn't see me.

'Who is it?' she said.

'It's me, Mrs Levy. Martin. Josie's nephew.'

There was no need for sirens when Hilda was around. She screamed and fell in a dead faint on the floor.

CHAPTER EIGHT

A House Full of Aunts

I'm in bed, listening to Auntie Minnie feed the chickens outside. I can hear the clucking sound she makes with her mouth. I can hear footsteps on the wooden stairs.

Uncle Ted is setting off to work. A house full of aunts and uncles! Life works out in funny ways sometimes.

Like the train crash. One of the orphan kids was on the train – Frank Chipping. His body was burnt so badly, no one could tell who it was. Poor kid. They reckon he was dead before he got burnt – I hope so.

Anyway, he wasn't meant to be on the train. I was, so Ted and Josie thought it was me. Poor old Ted tried to identify the body, but it was impossible. Frank was my age and size. They thought it had to be me. They were pretty cut-up about it.

Meanwhile, the real me was carted off to hospital.

They told me I had a great funeral. Even Hilda Levy was there. It's not surprising she got a shock when I turned up on her doorstep!

I'd better get up. Downstairs, Auntie Minnie is pouring out the tea. Josie is sorting out toast. They get on like a house on fire. So do Ted and Uncle Trevor. Uncle Ted has always wanted to go fishing. When he isn't working, that's what they do.

You're probably wondering by now, what's going on?

Ted and Josie hadn't found
anywhere to live. Then the railway
moved the repair work out of
London because of the bombing.
The new works were at Eastleigh,
between Winchester and
Southampton. The railway asked
Ted where he would like to go.

The day after my funeral Ted and
Josie looked for digs in Eastleigh.
They called in on Auntie Minnie
and Uncle Trevor. Auntie Minnie's
cottage had plenty of room. She
came up with the idea that they
stayed there for a bit. Then I turned
up. It's the summer now, and we're

all still here. Life's pretty good.

Yes, I've got two women to nag at me now. I don't really mind. Being in a big accident changes you. I don't want to get too soppy about this. The thing is, I never used to care what people felt about me. Now I know how they felt when they thought I was dead. It shakes you up a bit.

When the war's over I'm going back to London. I want to find the grave of that poor orphan kid who was me for a while. No one cared much for Frank Chipping, but I think of him a lot.

Sea Fever

by Gillian Philip

Saul loves the water. His dad hates it. Saul's mum walked into the sea and drowned. So Saul's dad moved them far away from the sea. But Saul still feels the pull of the water. Can he find a way back?

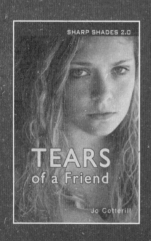

Tears of a Friend

by Jo Cotterill

Claire and Cassie have always been friends. But one day they have a huge row. They stop being friends. But then Claire faces a crisis and this is a real test: does Claire need Cassie anymore? Can they be friends?